MW01062282

Tales of Buttercup Grove

Sunflower Summer

By Wendy Dunham
Illustrated by Michal Sparks

HARVEST HOUSE PUBLISHERS
EUGENE, OREGON

The Scripture quotation on page 64 is from the *Holy Bible*, New Living Translation, copyright © 1996, 2004, 2007, 2013 by Tyndale House Foundation. Used by permission of Tyndale House Publishers, Inc., Carol Stream, Illinois 60188. All rights reserved.

Cover design by Mary Eakin

Interior design by Janelle Coury

Published in association with William K. Jensen Literary Agency, 119 Bampton Court, Eugene, Oregon 97404.

HARVEST KIDS is a registered trademark of The Hawkins Children's LLC. Harvest House Publishers, Inc., is the exclusive licensee of the federally registered trademark HARVEST KIDS.

SUNFLOWER SUMMER

Published by Harvest House Publishers
Eugene, Oregon 97402
www.harvesthousepublishers.com

ISBN 978-0-7369-7202-4 (hardcover)
ISBN 978-0-7369-7203-1 (eBook)

Library of Congress Cataloging-in-Publication Data
Names: Dunham, Wendy, author. | Sparks, Michal, illustrator.
Title: Sunflower summer / Wendy Dunham ; illustrations by Michal Sparks.
Description: Eugene Oregon : Harvest House Publishers, [2018] | Summary: Raccoon invites his friends to plant sunflower seeds to celebrate the first day of summer, but they must learn to be patient and wait for the plants to grow and bloom.
Identifiers: LCCN 2017016831 (print) | LCCN 2017035614 (ebook) | ISBN | ISBN 9780736972024 (hardcover) | ISBN 9780736972031 (eBook)
Subjects: | CYAC: Sunflowers—Fiction. | Gardening—Fiction. | Friendship—Fiction. | Animals—Fiction. | Summer—Fiction.
Classification: LCC PZ7.1.D86 (ebook) | LCC PZ7.1.D86 Sun 2018 (print) | DDC [E]—dc23
LC record available at https://lccn.loc.gov/2017016831

Printed in China

18 19 20 21 22 23 24 25 26 / RDS-JC / 10 9 8 7 6 5 4 3 2

1

First Day of Summer

Raccoon looked at his calendar.

It was the first day of summer.

"This is a good day to clean my garden shed," he said.

Raccoon swept the floor.

He dusted the cobwebs.

He stacked the flowerpots.

Then he found a pack of seeds.

He read the words on the front:

Giant Sunflower Seeds.

Raccoon opened the seeds.

He counted them.

There were seven.

"There are just enough seeds for my friends and me.

We should plant them to celebrate summer.

I will call my friends."

Raccoon called Skunk.

"Hello, Skunk," he said.
"Happy first day of summer."

“Happy first day of summer to you too,” said Skunk.

"We should celebrate the first day of summer," said Raccoon.

"Would you like to come to my house?"

"I would like that," said Skunk.

"I will call our other friends too," said Raccoon.

Raccoon called Mouse, Fox, Mole, Rabbit, and Beaver.

Soon everyone was at Raccoon's house.

"Happy first day of summer," said Raccoon.

"I found a pack of giant sunflower seeds," he said.

"We should plant them to celebrate summer."

"But there is no place to plant them," said Skunk. "There is no room in your garden. You have too many flowers."

"We can plant them at my house," said Fox.

"That is nice of you," said Raccoon.
"But your house is deep in
Buttercup Grove where it is shady.
And sunflowers need sun."

"We can plant them at my house," said Beaver. "My house is at the edge of Buttercup Grove. There is more sun near the edge."

"That is a good idea," said Raccoon.
"Let's go there now."

2

Planting Seeds

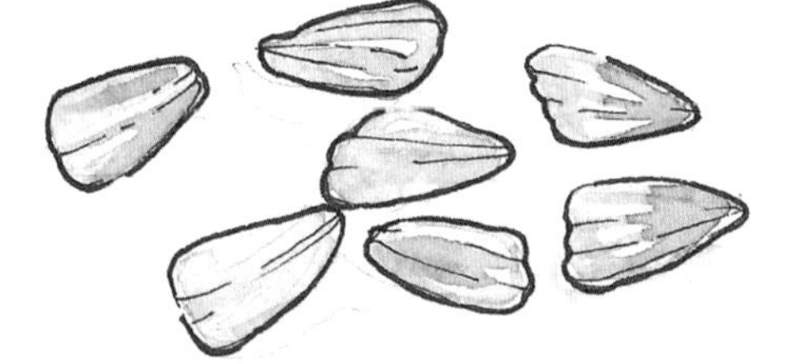

Raccoon, Skunk, Fox, Rabbit, and Beaver carried the shovels. Mouse and Mole carried the seeds.

Beaver was right. His yard was sunny.

"This is a perfect spot for sunflowers," said Raccoon. "There is a lot of sun here."

"Are they called sunflowers because they need sun to grow?" asked Skunk.

"They do need sun," said Raccoon. "But there is a special reason they are called sunflowers. You will find out when they are full-grown," said Raccoon.

Everyone wanted to know why, but
Raccoon would not tell.

He wanted them to be surprised.

Raccoon, Skunk, Fox, Rabbit, and Beaver
used shovels to get the dirt ready.
Mouse and Mole used their paws.

At first the dirt was hard.
When they finished, the dirt felt soft.

"Now we can dig holes for our seeds," said Raccoon. "We need seven holes."

“I am good at digging,” said Mole.
“I will dig the holes.”

“They must be one inch deep,”
said Raccoon.

"We have nothing to measure with," said Skunk. "Now we can't plant our seeds."

"I am one inch tall," said Mouse.
"The hole should be as tall as me."

Mole dug the first hole.

Mouse jumped in.

His head reached the top.

"That is just right," said Raccoon.
"Now the holes must be six inches apart,"
he said. "Who can measure that?"

Mouse raised his hand.

"If I roll six times in a row that will be six inches."

"You are very smart," said Rabbit.

Mouse bent down at the first hole.

He rolled six times.

Mole dug a new hole where Mouse stopped. Mouse and Mole worked together until there were seven holes.

"Now we are ready to plant our seeds," said Raccoon.

Everyone put their seed in a hole. They covered them with dirt.

"Now we will water our seeds," said Raccoon.

"We cannot water our seeds," said Skunk.
"We do not have a watering can."

"I will make one," said Beaver. "I have a tin can. I will use my teeth to poke holes in it."

"That is a good idea," said Rabbit.

Everyone took turns watering their seeds. Then they sat and waited. And they waited. And they waited some more.

"The seeds are not growing," said Skunk. "What is taking so long?"

"I will read the directions," said Raccoon. He read them out loud. "Giant sunflower seeds sprout in seven days. They will be full-grown in one hundred days."

"Seven days until they sprout?" shouted Skunk. "That is too long!"

“One hundred days until they are full-grown?” shouted Rabbit.
“We cannot wait one hundred days!
We will be old by then!”

Raccoon laughed. "We will not be old. But we must be patient. One hundred days will be at the end of summer. We can watch them grow all summer long."

“That is a long time,” said Skunk.

All summer long Skunk, Raccoon, Beaver, Mole, Mouse, Fox, and Rabbit took care of their giant sunflowers.

They watered them.
They weeded them.
And they watched them grow.

3

One Hundred Days

When the sunflowers were one hundred days old, Raccoon, Skunk, Beaver, Mouse, Mole, Fox, and Rabbit had a celebration.

They packed three picnics. One picnic for breakfast. One picnic for lunch. And one picnic for supper. They spent the whole day watching their sunflowers.

When they ate breakfast,
Skunk noticed something.
"Look," he said, "the sunflowers
are facing east. They must like
watching the sun rise."

When they ate lunch, Fox noticed something. "Look," he said, "the sunflowers are looking straight up. That is where the sun is."

"I wonder what they are looking at," said Mouse.

"Maybe they are watching the clouds," said Mole.

But Raccoon just smiled.

After they ate supper, Beaver noticed something. "Look," he said, "now the sunflowers are facing west."

"They must be watching the sun set," said Skunk. "If they like watching the sun rise and set, maybe they like the sun."

"They do," said Raccoon. "Sunflowers like the sun very much. They turn their faces to the sun and follow it all day long."

"That is why they are called sunflowers!" shouted Skunk. "What a special flower!"

"Yes," said Raccoon,
"they are a special flower."

"They took a very long time to grow," said Skunk. "But I am glad we waited."

"If we look forward to
something we don't yet have,
we must wait patiently and confidently."

Romans 8:25